Produced by Kroha Associates, Inc.
Middletown, Connecticut.

Printed in the United States of America.

ISBN 1-56326-107-3

A Promise
Is A Promise

By Ruth Lerner Perle

One hot summer day, Minnie and Lilly went over to Daisy's house. "Let's play checkers," Minnie suggested.

"Great idea!" Daisy said. "But I don't remember where I put them. I know they must be here somewhere."

Minnie and Lilly helped Daisy look for the game. They looked in the drawers, on the shelves, and in the toy chest, but the checkers were nowhere to be found.

"Well, never mind," Lilly said. "It's too hot to play indoors anyway. Let's play Frisbee in the yard."

"Okay!" Daisy said. "But I'll have to look for my Frisbee. I'm not so sure where I put it." The girls looked everywhere, and finally Minnie spotted the Frisbee under Daisy's desk.

"How did the Frisbee end up there?" Lilly asked.

"I guess I forgot to put it away," said Daisy.

Daisy opened her closet door. "Now all I have to do is find a top that's cool to wear and then we can go out to play," she said.

Daisy looked on all the hangers. No top. Then she looked on all the hooks. No top. She looked on all the closet shelves, too, but still no top.

Finally, Daisy searched on the floor behind the shoes and sneakers. There, in a heap, was the top — at last!

"Well, I'm ready to go now," Daisy said.

Lilly looked at her watch. "I'm afraid it's too late for me to play now. I promised to meet Clarabelle at the library," she said. "Maybe we'll play Frisbee another time."

Lilly said good-bye and left.

"I'll have to be going, too," Minnie said.

"That's too bad! I'm sorry I took so much time," Daisy told her.

"You know, Daisy," Minnie said, "if you straightened out your room a little, it would be easier to find things — and besides, it would look so much prettier."

Daisy looked around her room. "I've been meaning to clean it up," she said. "But I never know where to start, and it's a lot of work for just one person."

"I'll be glad to help you!" Minnie said. "It's too late to do it today, but I'll come here first thing tomorrow morning and we'll clean up your room together."

"Oh, Minnie! Will you really? That would be so great!" Daisy shouted.

"I just hope it will be a little cooler," Minnie said as she waved good-bye to her friend.

The next day was sticky, hot, and humid. Minnie was getting ready to go to Daisy's house when the telephone rang. It was Clarabelle.

"Hi, Minnie," Clarabelle said. "It's so hot! Would you like to come over and swim in my pool?"

Minnie really wanted to say yes. She would have loved to cool off. But instead she said, "Thank you, Clarabelle. I would really love to, but I promised I'd help Daisy clean her room."

"Well, why don't you help her tomorrow?" Clarabelle asked.

"A promise is a promise," Minnie answered. "I don't want to disappoint Daisy."

Minnie hung up and just then, Penny called.
"My mom is driving us to the beach today, and you're invited,"
she said. "It's a perfect beach day."
"I'm sorry, Penny, but I already made plans," said Minnie.

After she turned down Penny's invitation, Minnie left for Daisy's house. On the way, she passed by Clarabelle's yard. She could see Clarabelle sitting in her pool with Lilly. They were splashing and laughing and having a good time.

Minnie continued on her way. When she stopped on the corner, she heard *honk! honk!* It was Penny and her mother and some other girls on their way to the beach.

Penny waved and called to Minnie. "We'll miss you!"

"Have fun!" Minnie called back to them.

When Minnie arrived at Daisy's house, Daisy had a cold pitcher of lemonade waiting for her.

"Oh, Minnie! I'm so glad you're here to help me. I know it's a terrible day to be working," she said.

Minnie took a sip of lemonade. Then she smiled and said, "Okay, let's get going. The sooner we start, the sooner we'll be finished."

The two girls went upstairs, turned on their favorite music tape, and started to work.

First, they picked up all the toys that were lying around and put them in the toy chest.

Then they hung all of Daisy's pretty dresses on hangers and put them neatly in the closet.

Next, they
straightened
out the dresser
drawers.

Then they made the bed, smoothed the bedspread,
and arranged the pillows neatly against the headboard.

Minnie looked around the room. "Well, it looks much better already!" she said. "Now all we have to do is dust and sweep the floor."

When Minnie started to sweep under the bed, her broom hit something. She looked to see what it was.

"Hurray! Look what I found!" she cried. "It's the box of checkers!" There were other lost treasures under the bed, too: a jump rope, a ball, shoe laces, slippers, and a doll's sweater.

"I was wondering where all these things disappeared to," Daisy said. "They've been lost for so long, I forgot I had them."

Soon everything was clean and tidy. The two girls smiled. "Thank you for helping, Minnie. I could never have done this without you," Daisy said. "It's a good thing you had nothing else to do today."

"Let's get washed up," Minnie said. "Then we can play a game of checkers."

"I have an idea. We can clean up under the sprinkler in the yard. It will be fun and we can cool off at the same time," Daisy said. "I'll get some bathing suits. Now I know just where to find them!" she added with a grin.

Daisy opened her dresser drawer and took out a bathing suit for each of them.

The two girls went out into the yard and turned on the sprinkler.
They ran and splashed and had a great time.

Later that afternoon, while they were playing checkers, Daisy saw Penny coming back from the beach. Daisy waved to her friend and called, "Gee, I sure wish I could have gone to the beach today!"

"I would have invited you, but Minnie told me you two were going to clean your room," Penny said.

"You missed a fun time, Minnie," Penny continued. "It's too bad you didn't come."

"I would have enjoyed it, but I had a promise to keep," Minnie said, winking at Daisy.

After Penny left, Daisy said, "I'll bet you really wanted to go to the beach today, Minnie. It means a lot to me that you kept your promise to me instead. You're the greatest!"

Going to the beach would have been fun. But keeping that promise I made to Daisy made me feel really good inside!

This book belongs to:

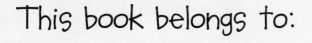

....

....

....

Retold by Gaby Goldsack
Illustrated by Ruth Galloway (Advocate)
Designed by Jester Designs

Language consultant: Betty Root

ISBN 1-40545-557-8

This is a Parragon Publishing book
This edition published in 2006

Parragon Publishing
Queen Street House
4 Queen Street
Bath BA1 1HE, UK

Copyright © Parragon Books Ltd 2002

Printed in India

The Gingerbread Man

Helping Your Child Read

Learning to read is an exciting challenge for most children. From a very early age, sharing storybooks with children, talking about the pictures, and guessing what might happen next are all very important parts of the reading experience.

Sharing Reading

Set aside a regular quiet time to share reading with younger children, or to be available to encourage older children as they develop into independent readers.

First Readers are intended to encourage and support the early stages of learning to read. They present well-loved tales that children will enjoy hearing again and again. Familiarity helps children identify some of the words and phrases.

When you feel your child is ready to move ahead, encourage him or her to join in so that you read the story aloud together. Always pause to talk about the pictures. The easy-to-read speech bubbles in **First Readers** provide an excellent 'joining-in' activity. The bright, clear illustrations and matching text will help children understand the story.

Building Confidence

In time, children will want to read *to* you. When this happens, be patient and give continual praise. They may not read all the words correctly, but children's substitutions are often very good guesses.

The repetition in each book is especially helpful for building confidence. If your child cannot read a particular word, go back to the beginning of the sentence and read it together so the meaning is not lost. Most important, do not continue if your child is tired or just needs a break.

Reading alone

The next step is to ask your child to read alone. Try to be on hand to give help and support. Remember to give lots of encouragement and praise.

Along with other simple stories, **First Readers** will ensure that children will find reading an enjoyable and rewarding experience.

Once upon a time there was a little old man and a little old woman.

One day the little old woman made a gingerbread man.

The little old woman put the gingerbread man in the oven to bake. The little old woman and the little old man waited.

Then the little old man opened the oven. Out jumped the gingerbread man.

Let me out!

Oh dear!

He ran off, singing
"Run, run, as fast as you can,
You can't catch me,
I'm the gingerbread man."

The gingerbread man ran on until he met a cow.

"Stop!" said the cow. "I want to eat you."

"I have run away from a little old man and a little old woman," laughed the gingerbread man. "And I can run away from you."

"Run, run, as fast as you can,
You can't catch me,
I'm the gingerbread man."

The gingerbread man ran on until he met a horse.

"Stop!" said the horse. "I want to eat you."

"I have run away from a little old man, a little old woman, and a cow," laughed the gingerbread man. "And I can run away from you."

"Run, run, as fast as you can,
You can't catch me,
I'm the gingerbread man."

The gingerbread man ran on until he met a farmer.

"Stop!" said the farmer. "I want to eat you."

"I have run away from a little old man, a little old woman, a cow, and a horse," laughed the gingerbread man. "And I can run away from you."

Come back!

He ran so fast that the farmer could not catch him.

"Run, run, as fast as you can,

You can't catch me,

I'm the gingerbread man."

The gingerbread man ran on and on.

He was very proud of his running.

"No one can catch me," he said.

I can run fast!

Then he met a sly old fox. "Come here!"
said the fox. "I want to talk to you."

"I have run away from a little old man, a little old woman, a cow, a horse, and a farmer," laughed the gingerbread man. "And I can run away from you.

Oh yes! You can run fast!

"Run, run, as fast as you can,

You can't catch me,

I'm the gingerbread man."

I can run away from you!

The fox ran after the gingerbread man.
The gingerbread man ran even faster.

Soon they came to a river. "How will
I cross the river?" asked the
gingerbread man.

"Jump on my tail. I will take you across," said the sly old fox.

The gingerbread man jumped onto the fox's tail.

The fox began to swim across the river.

Splash!

Soon he said to the gingerbread man, "My tail is tired. Jump onto my back."

So the gingerbread man did.

Jump on my back!

Then the fox said, "My back is tired.

Jump onto my nose."

So the gingerbread man did.

Soon they reached the other side. The fox threw the gingerbread man into the air.

Snap!

Then, gulp, he ate the gingerbread man in a single bite.

The gingerbread man
never ran away again.

Read and Say

How many of these words can you say?
The pictures will help you. Look back in
your book and see if you can find the
words in the story.

farmer

cow

fox

gingerbread man

horse

man

oven

river

woman

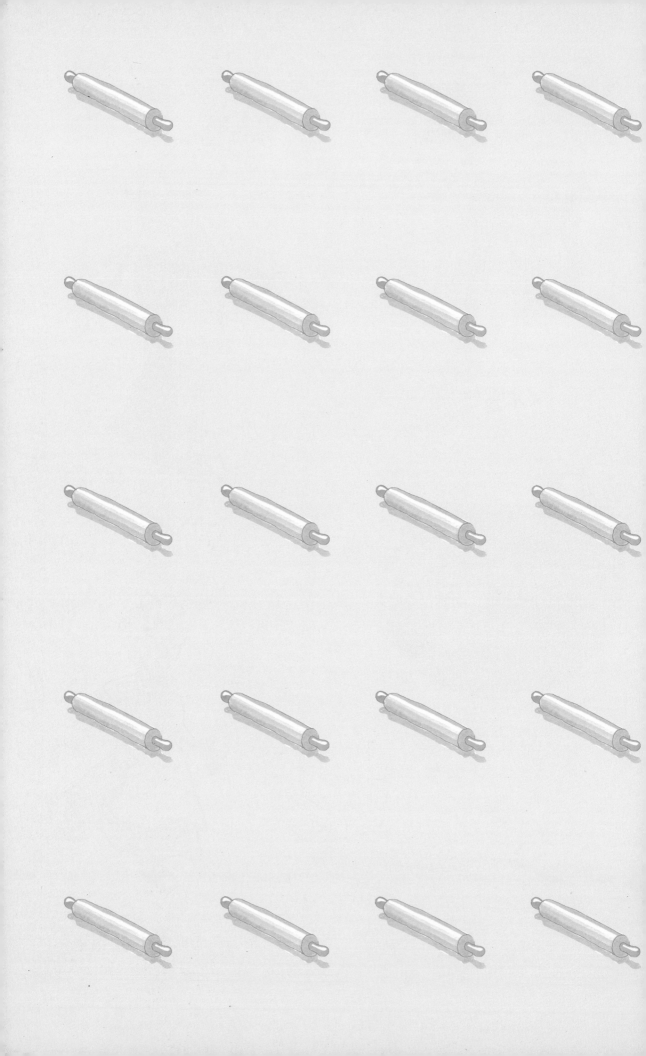